I AM GYPSY

Other Books By Cap Daniels

Chase Fulton Novels
Book One: The Opening Chase
Book Two: The Broken Chase
Book Three: The Stronger Chase
Book Four: The Unending Chase
Book Five: The Distant Chase
Book Six: The Entangled Chase
Book Seven: The Devil's Chase
Book Eight: The Angel's Chase
Book Nine: The Forgotten Chase
Book Ten: The Emerald Chase
Book Eleven: The Polar Chase
Book Twelve: The Burning Chase
Book Thirteen: The Poison Chase (February 2021)

We Were Brave

The Chase Is On (Novella)

I AM GYPSY

CAP DANIELS

ANCHOR WATCH
PUBLISHING
** USA **

I Am Gypsy
Cap Daniels

This is a work of fiction. Names, characters, places, historical events, and incidents are the product of the author's imagination or have been use fictitiously. Although many locations such as marinas, airports, hotels, restaurants, and buildings used in this work actually exist, they are used fictitiously and may have been relocated, exaggerated, or otherwise modified by creative license for the purpose of this work. Although many characters are based on character traits, physical attributes, skills, or intellect of actual individuals, all of the characters in this work are products of the author's imagination.

Published by:

ANCHOR WATCH
——— PUBLISHING ———
** USA **

13 Digit ISBN: 978-1-7323024-6-4
Library of Congress Control Number: 2018912763

Cover Design: German Creative

Dedication

This book is dedicated to...
The thousands of people who lost so much to the ravages of Hurricane
Michael on October 10, 2018 in the Panhandle of Florida.

AND

The proceeds of this book will be used to directly benefit those individuals, families, and small businesses impacted by Hurricane Michael.

I Am Gypsy

CAP DANIELS

Chapter 1
Tuesday

I am Gypsy. I was born in November of 1981 in Florida, the Sunshine State. I think it was a Tuesday afternoon when I first saw the sunshine, smelled the salt air, and felt the Gulf of Mexico welcome me into the world. I'm a sailing yacht. That probably sounds a little pretentious, so just think of me as a boat instead of a yacht. After all, there's nothing shameful about being a boat. I'm rather proud being one . . . or more correctly, I *was* proud of being one. Let me tell you about my life, and especially about how it ended on a Wednesday.

I remember now. It was definitely a Tuesday when I splashed into the water for the first time. I didn't know anything about the world, and all I knew about people was that they had created me. It all started in the brilliant mind of a guy named John. He's the man who dreamed me up and drew the first sketches of me. Those sketches became detailed drawings and plans, and then a bunch of men—and a few women, too—went to work molding fiberglass and laying my keel. There had been two hundred eighty before me who looked almost exactly like me, but I was number two hundred eighty-one. I heard a rumor once that I was the middle child because they made about two hundred fifty more just like me after I was born, so I wasn't anything special back then. But that all changed.

Unlike orphan boats that sit in a marina or on a boatyard for months, or sometimes even years before someone comes to take them home, I already had a home. Someone very special had been waiting for months, just for me. In fact, it wasn't just someone; it was a whole family who'd been waiting for me. I think they were the first people I'd ever seen who were happy to see me. Don't get me wrong. The men and women who built me liked me well enough, but I was just a few weeks' work to them. You see, I was a production yacht . . . um, I mean boat. I learned later in life that there are custom boats built specifically the way an owner wants, with paint and interior picked out months ahead of time. That wasn't me; I was just a regular old boat. But to that family standing on the dock, I was a dream come true. The day I met my family was a great day.

We had sea trials. I didn't know what sea trials were back then. Remember, I was just a baby. All I knew was that I had an instinct to *go*. Sort of like when a sheepdog puppy just knows how to herd the sheep, or when a Labrador retriever can't wait to bring back a ball. It was like that. I knew I was supposed to be out on the ocean and in the wind. I knew I was supposed to *go*. And that family couldn't wait to *go* with me.

We motored out of the marina, and I didn't like that at all. The diesel engine was loud and hot. I remember thinking there had to be a better way to *go* than putting up with that hot, noisy, smelly diesel engine. And I was right. There was a much better way. After thirty minutes of turning me this way and that, backing up and going forward, I earned my wings. My wings were a pair of sails: beautiful, billowing white sails that slid up my mast and forestay and made me look like an elegant lady ready for the ball. When those sails went up and the diesel fell silent, that's the moment I was truly born.

Thomas was his name. He was a quiet man; the kind of man who thought a lot more than he spoke. I learned those kinds of men were rare, but far better than the kinds of men who spoke more than they thought. I liked the way Thomas seemed to want to work with me instead of trying to make me do things I didn't want to do. Even though I can't really talk, he listened to me. Thomas and I developed a language all our own. When I'd heel a little too far and my rigging would creak and moan, Thomas would shorten my sails and take some of the stress off of me. When I was unable to keep my sails from luffing, Thomas would turn slightly away from the wind so my sails would fill again. He'd always pat my wheel and apologize for letting us get too close to the wind.

That's a bizarre concept: sailing too close to the wind. We sail-boats—and sailing yachts, too—love the wind, but we all have our limitations. None of us can sail directly into the wind. Some of the fancy racing boats can sail a lot closer to the wind than I can, but I can sail about thirty degrees off the wind. If Thomas tried to sail me any closer to the wind than thirty degrees, I'd stand up, slow down, and my sails would flutter and stop making the lift I needed to *go*. That fluttering in my sails is called luffing. There are a lot of goofy words for things I do that don't make any sense. We'll talk about some of those along the way, but for now, I want to tell you more about Thomas.

Thomas married a beautiful woman named Terry, and they made two of the most adorable children in the world: a boy and a girl. Tommy was fun, but he was mean sometimes. He was one of those people who talked more than he thought, and we all know how I feel about that. The little girl was Tina, and she was perfect. She had her mother's blue eyes and blonde hair that floated on the wind. She'd giggle and point at everything that moved, and she loved the dolphins. So did I.

There was something special about dolphins. They were smart and mischievous . . . kind of like Tommy was. They were so much fun to watch, and they seemed to like me, too. They'd swim along-side me and play in my bow wakes, the little waves I'd make when we were sailing. The water curled and twinkled in the sunlight. The waves weren't very big, but the dolphins liked to surf in them, and sometimes, when everything was just right, a dolphin would brush up against me just to say hi. And I loved that. Mine was a good life in those early days.

I got to watch Tommy and Tina grow up, and Thomas and I taught them to sail.

"Look for the wind," Thomas would say, pointing across the water. "You can't actually see the wind. You can only see the results of the wind, but it's there. Feel it on your face and look up at the Windex."

The rest of the world calls the little plastic arrow on top of my mast a *weather vane*, but not sailors. They call it a *Windex*. They have to be different.

"Yeah, yeah, Dad. I get it. Now let me drive."

That was Tommy, of course. He never slowed down.

"Shh. Listen. Do you hear that?" Tina closed her eyes and aimed her right ear toward my headsail. "It's talking to us. It needs our attention."

She was the thinker and the listener.

Before my sails luffed, they started making sounds they shouldn't make. In fact, sails shouldn't make any sounds when properly trimmed. Tina could hear them complaining before they luffed.

"Bear away from the wind, Tommy." Tina pulled at the wheel.

"No! Shut up! I'm driving!"

Yep, that's Tommy again, but hey, don't get on his case too much. He was just a boy, and boys do dumb stuff like yelling at their sisters and never listening when they should. And they always want to do it their way. Maybe Tommy would grow out of doing dumb things, but I hoped Tina never changed.

They spent almost every weekend with me. We'd sail someplace, drop my anchor, and other than actually *going*, that was my favorite time of all. They would cook and eat and laugh and talk about things. They all had dreams. Thomas wanted to retire and move to the Cayman Islands. Who doesn't? Terry's dreams were different. I never remember her talking about what she wanted for herself. Her dream was for her children to grow up and be happy, healthy, and successful, and to have families of their own. She wanted things for other people, but not for herself. What an amazing way to think . . . and feel . . . and be.

Tommy's dream won't be any big surprise. He wanted to be a racecar driver.

Hey, look at that. Race car is spelled the same backward and forward. There's some crazy, non-sailing-related word for that. Give me just a minute, and it'll come to me. Wait! It's a *palindrome*. I knew I'd get it.

Tina dreamed of being a princess when she grew up. I wish I could've told her that she was already a princess and to never grow out of that, but I couldn't, and sadly, she did.

Tommy would climb every part of me he could reach while Tina and Thomas counted stars and made up stories about each of them. Terry cleaned my galley and quietly sang songs that I loved. She cared so much for my interior. She kept me clean and always seemed happy and content seeing her family enjoying themselves and each other.

Meanwhile, I lay quietly at anchor, letting the waves lap against my hull, while I gently rolled with the subtle movement of the ocean. Tina always fell asleep first. She would curl up into a tiny ball, taking up no more space than a pillow, and sleep silently for hours on end. I cradled and protected her as she slept. She was my favorite.

Tommy would bounce around until he was exhausted, and then he'd collapse wherever his body ran out of energy. He even slept fitfully, tossing and turning and talking in gibberish that no one could understand. I loved him, too, because like me, he wanted to *go*.

Thomas and Terry always double-checked my anchor and made sure the anchor light, high atop my mast, was lit before crawling into their cabin in my bow. They always whispered *I love you* before falling asleep. I knew they were talking to each other, but sometimes I let myself believe they were talking to me.

Sometimes, they made love quietly and softly. They kissed and caressed each other, sharing themselves tenderly, always careful to make sure the children were sound asleep. In these times, I closed my eyes. Those moments were uniquely theirs, and I silently protected them while they loved each other.

Thomas was always awake first. He'd brew coffee and walk my deck, making sure everything was exactly as it should be. He took such loving care of me. The love Terry showed me in my interior was equaled by the diligence Thomas demonstrated in caring for my hull and rigging. He was meticulous and careful, never forceful. I think he knew how hard I worked to keep his family safe and comfortable, so he returned the favor with unrelenting care. If I was dirty, he washed me. If part of me was worn or frayed, he quickly replaced that part. Sometimes, when no one else was around, he'd stand and look at me, slowly nodding and offering a satisfied smile. I so wish I could've spoken with him. I would've thanked him a thousand times, just like he thanked me for always bringing them home safely. I had a good family. And I was a good boat.

Chapter 2
Wednesday

Time passed relentlessly. Weeks turned into months and years, and my family didn't always spend weekends with me anymore. I was comfortable, though. I was in a nice marina with other boats and families. When my family did come, it wasn't the same.

Thomas still walked my decks, but instead of the careful attention with which he used to work on my rigging, he began sending other people to do the work.

"Every time we come down here, there's something else that needs fixing," he'd say.

I didn't like disappointing him, but I was helpless. I liked living in the marina, but it was hard on me. I was over a dozen years old, and the wind and waves drove me against the dock and pulled on my rigging. I wasn't breaking on purpose, but sometimes, I thought Thomas believed it was my fault.

We didn't go out and anchor anymore. We didn't cook and laugh and count stars. We'd go on day sails sometimes, but they were always too short. Tommy had baseball and Tina had soccer. Whatever those things are. Thomas had meetings, and Terry was tired and had headaches that crippled her. I don't know what a headache is like, but I understand being crippled.

Sometimes Tommy came to see me with some of his friends. I didn't like that at all. They never wanted to *go*. They just wanted to drink and smoke and listen to loud music. I felt so dirty when they left. I wanted Terry to come take care of me.

Tina came sometimes. She was always alone. She would sit on my bow and listen. Sometimes she would sing barely above a whisper, just like Terry used to do. The little princess was becoming a beautiful woman just like her mother had been when I was born.

My family was growing older and growing apart. I remember wondering why they'd always been together as if they were dependent upon each other for life. They seemed to thrive from being together and loving each other, and from spending time with me, but all of that was changing.

I don't know where they went when we weren't together. Maybe they had another boat somewhere. Maybe someday I'd get to see it. Maybe they had a real home and other people who relied on them for things. Maybe I wasn't as important to them anymore. Maybe their other boat was better, and I was getting older like my family. Was I changing, too?

Tina came late one afternoon while it was raining. The rain felt good on my deck. It cleaned me and kept me cool. Tina was wearing a black dress and had tears streaked down her beautiful face. She climbed aboard and sat behind my wheel, sobbing and gasping as the rain softly fell.

"Bear away from the wind, Tommy."

She choked on the words, and I couldn't understand what was happening to her. I remembered the many times she'd try to teach Tommy to listen to and work with me instead of trying so hard to force me to do things I couldn't do. I couldn't understand why she was then repeating herself when no one else was there, and I couldn't understand why she was in so much pain.

Like always, she was alone, but somehow, she seemed more alone than usual. Her tears wouldn't stop falling, and she lay on my bow with her face in her hands while the rain fell on her beautiful black dress. Her soaked hair looked dark and lifeless pressed against her skin. It looked nothing like the golden, wind-blown hair I'd so loved seeing dancing in the breeze.

"Why, God? Why? Why couldn't it be me?" She pounded on my deck with her fists and screamed into the strengthening rain.

What was she talking about? Why was she so angry?

She crawled from the deck and into my main salon. Rainwater poured from her dress and hair, but she seemed not to notice it. Her tears were still coming in sheets, just like the rain.

I began to believe the rain I had enjoyed was actually the whole world crying with Tina. I'd never seen such sadness and anger. I wanted to cradle her. I wanted her to curl into that tiny ball and sleep silently and peacefully in my embrace. She had come to me for comfort, and I couldn't do anything. I was helpless and sad. I think she must have felt the same, but I had no idea why.

I watched her pull a wine bottle from the rack in my galley and clumsily force the corkscrew into the top. She tried wiping the tears from her eyes, but it was no use. She was broken and torn apart on the inside. Someone or something had hurt her, or someone or something had been taken from her. Again, I longed for words but had none.

She sat on my cabin sole and drank from the bottle. The crimson wine trickled from the corners of her mouth and left blood-like stains on her delicate skin. Her sobbing gave way to gasping, and finally to the deep, prolonged breaths of exhausted sleep.

I tried to cradle her, but my cabin sole was rigid and cold. I couldn't comfort her body—or her soul. I ached to whisper to her that it would all be okay. I longed to stroke her hair and dry her tears, but I could not.

The rain stopped, and the moon shone through the parting clouds. It cast long shadows on my deck and shone through my hatch, lighting Tina's once beautiful and delicate face—the face her mother had worn a decade and a half before, the face that was now stained with wine and tears and twisted into misshapen, heart-broken agony. And I remained lost and powerless to help my family.

"Tina! Tina! Are you in there?"

Thomas was there!

His heavy footfalls on my deck felt foreign and angry. He burst through the companionway and down the stairs.

"Tina! What are you doing? You scared the hell out of your mother!"

It was anger. I'd never seen Thomas angry. It made me feel ashamed and small. I wanted to hide. The man who'd shown such patience and tenderness to me and our family was now raging and furious. I didn't recognize him, and he ignored me. Never had he ignored me. Nothing made sense, and I was afraid and had so many questions.

"Daddy, stop it. I'm fine." She wiped at her eyes and pulled away from him.

"You're not fine. Look at yourself! You're drunk. You're lying on the floor. And you're soaking wet! You can't do this to your mother."

"What about me, Daddy? What about me? What do you think this does to me?" Her tears were back, and an angry cloud hid the moon, draining the life from the earth.

"Listen to me." Thomas grabbed his daughter's arms, lifted her from the sole, and placed her gently on the settee. "This is hard on all of us. It's the worst thing that could happen, but we're still a family and we have to face this together."

The gentleness and patience I'd always known from him had returned, but what was he talking about? What could possibly be the worst thing that could happen? I wanted to understand. I wanted to comfort them. I needed to help my family.

Tina hugged her father, and they cried together, sobbing and clinging to each other as if their lives depended on the embrace. I tried to reach up and hold them. I tried to caress them. I tried, but I was helpless and still confused.

They left, and I was alone and still consumed with questions without answers and fears without understanding. Where had they gone? What had hurt my family so deeply? What had driven Thomas to such anger, and Tina to such depths of despair?

I could taste the salty tears of my family on the cushion of my settee and on the wood of my cabin sole. I could still hear their sobs and gasps. I felt an emptiness I couldn't explain. It was deeper than simply not having my family aboard; it was more like I'd never have them aboard again. It was strong, and it was painful.

The moon didn't show again that night, but the sun finally rose over the eastern sky. Dolphins chased baitfish behind my rudder, and pelicans dived on the same prey. Neither was successful. As the sun warmed the moist morning air, the wind seemed to blow from directly overhead. It felt heavy and wrong. Everything felt wrong.

My family came, and nothing was ever right again. Thomas came first with Tina a few feet behind him, and Terry followed. Their faces were stained with tears, just as Tina's had been the night before. Terry labored over each step she took as if her feet weighed more than she could move—as if her body were sinking into the earth.

Without a word, Thomas cast off my mooring lines and started my diesel. I still hated the sound of the engine, but I hated the silence of my family even more.

The wind was blowing, yet we motored on as if no one aboard had the will or strength to unfurl my sails and let me *go*. It was a cold, painful feeling, and I still couldn't divine the answers to my questions.

Finally, my anchor fell in the cove where we'd spent so many nights eating, laughing, counting stars, and singing. My engine fell silent, and my family—Thomas, Terry, and Tina—stood on my deck beside my shrouds.

Thomas held Terry's hand and Terry held Tina's.

Choking back tears, Thomas said, "We thought this is where you'd want to be, son. This is where our family spent so many hours . . . some of the happiest hours of our lives. Now that you're gone, we fear our happiness can never return. But we wanted you to return here, to our family's spot. We love you, Tommy, and our lives will never again be complete without you."

He opened a brass urn and poured Tommy's ashes into the wind. The gray powder that had been Tommy—part of my family, part of me—drifted onto the water and became lost in the ocean. Everyone wept. Even me.

Chapter 3
Thursday

I would never know how Tommy died, but knowing I would spend my life in the same water that held his remains made me feel like he was still part of me. Tommy's death made me consider the day *my* life would end. Would I be run down by a freighter on the open ocean? Would I perish in a fire? Would I open up and take enough of the ocean inside me that I would fall to the murky depths, never to see the sun or feel the wind again?

I learned that dying isn't the worst thing that can happen. Sometimes living is worse. Living, after all, is dying slowly. Some thrive for decades, and then succumb to age or illness, and drift quietly into darkness. Others, like Tommy, live fearlessly and ferociously until life is suddenly ripped from their bodies far too early, and with far too much grief poured onto their families. The worst, though, is dying a little more every day in the wake of unthinkable tragedy. That is what I learned from my first family.

I was two decades distant from the day I first met my family. Tina was perhaps two decades and two years from the day she first drew a breath. And Thomas and Terry were, I suppose, twice that distant from their births. Time isn't a concept I've ever understood. The moon endlessly circles us, and we endlessly circle the sun. I wonder if it ever ends.

My family came and brought things of every sort. They brought clothes, food, books, and even a guitar. I'd seen guitars and even heard the sounds they make. Sometimes they were pleasant, but only sometimes. Maybe everyone has a guitar somewhere . . . maybe.

Thomas filled my water tanks with fresh water and my diesel tank with clean fuel. We were *going*, and I was happy. I'd wanted to *go* since the first breeze I ever felt. I'd missed *going* as time passed and as my family grew older, and especially since Tommy had gone on to wherever people go after this.

My shore power cord was disconnected, coiled, and stowed away. My dock lines were brought aboard and also coiled and stowed. We weren't just *going*. We were going away.

The ocean and sky welcomed us. The wind blew and the sea was calm. I was free. My sails were stretched and full. My hull was slicing through the blue ocean and dolphins were dancing with me. I was happy on the outside, but the inside wasn't the same.

It wasn't the same without Tommy. Terry didn't care for me the way she had before. She still cleaned me, but she never sang, and her touch was hard. She read a Bible and cried every night. Her once flawless skin drew up as if the life was slowly escaping her face, leaving her withered and dried. Perhaps it was the tears. Perhaps she needed the tears to stay inside her . . . perhaps.

Tina tried to pretend she was happy. She let her hair fly in the wind, and she still stared into the heavens at night, but she no longer counted the stars. She just stared as if she wished she could be among the stars, or perhaps with Tommy . . . perhaps.

Thomas busied himself with meaningless tasks. I had so many parts that needed his attention and love, but he created chores that had no value or benefit to him or me. It was as if he just needed to be doing something with his hands. He didn't whisper to Terry that he loved her. He no longer reached for her in the dark. He no longer told his daughter stories under the stars. Perhaps he felt he wasn't the man his wife needed, or the father his daughter had once adored since Tommy had been taken . . . perhaps.

We sailed southward toward the sun and toward the imaginary line dividing the Earth in half. It has a name, and I'll remember in time. The waters warmed, and the air thickened with heaviness . . . with humidity and energy. Great whales swam beneath my keel, and I saw things I'd never imagined. Fish of every shape, size, and color danced beneath me, and some even leapt from the water beside me as if they wanted to see my family.

Tina played the guitar softly at night. It made a sad, mournful sound that must've been the pieces of her soul escaping through the guitar. She mindlessly fingered the strings as if the sadness of the song drove itself and dragged her hands along, forcing them to pluck out the pain of every note until sleep—merciful sleep—enraptured her body.

She no longer lay in a ball, but her body reclined limply and awkwardly in restless slumber. She was no longer the child I had loved or the princess she pretended to be. Her eyes were empty, and her smile was gone, but to me, she'd always be that beautiful little girl and that perfect princess.

The sun filled the sky six times before I saw land again. I didn't think I'd be happy to stop *going*, but I was. Perhaps the sadness of my family and their emptiness had finally fallen upon me, as well. The joy of the wind in my sails, and the dolphins dancing at my bow, grew shallow, and I felt alone. I couldn't understand how I could feel loneliness without being alone. Perhaps that's exactly what my family was feeling. Although they were still alive and together, they were distant from each other by fathoms, by oceans, by worlds, and I was but a material thing to them. I had lost the life I'd once held, and so had my family.

Thomas tied me into a slip in a marina like I'd never seen. There were so many boats and so many people. So much was happening. I was overwhelmed. He connected my shore power, and I felt the electricity course through me, but I couldn't feel the love of my family—that was gone, and that was what I wanted to feel most of all. I was so far from home and still confused.

Thomas and Terry stepped ashore with their bags in their arms and stared at me for a long time. Tina stood in my main salon with her arms wrapped around my mast and tears in her eyes. "I'm going to miss you, Gypsy."

Miss me? What are you talking about? Wait a minute. What's happening?

I watched her climb the stairs and step through the companionway. She turned and closed my hatch before sliding her arm through the strap of her guitar case and stepping onto the dock. She didn't look back. None of them did. My family walked away and left me tied up in a marina far from home, and they never looked back.

The night came, and the sounds were different. People were everywhere. Boats came and went, and the hordes of people kept coming in wave after wave.

Some were happy and young, holding hands and singing. Some were drunk and alone in a crowd. Some were just as confused as I was, not knowing where they were or what would happen next. It was chaos, and I was right in the middle of it.

The darkness wore on until finally the people disappeared. A few remained, but they were quiet and still. I relaxed and thought about my family. Perhaps they'd be back soon . . . perhaps not.

The sun arose again and it got hot. A man with no shoes, no shirt, and hair that looked like it was tied in knots, hopped over my starboard lifeline and galloped down the stairs. He looked into my bilge and even opened the hatch to my diesel. Maybe he was there to remove the hot, noisy, stinky thing. No such luck. He checked the oil and coolant and tugged on the belts. He closed the hatch and flipped on my electronics. I never really knew what the electronics were for. People looked at them with great interest, especially when we were far from land, but I always found my way without looking at them.

The man whistled incessantly. I don't think he was whistling any particular song, but he seemed content—even though his hair looked painfully knotted.

"Let's see what you can do, *Gypsy Girl.*"

Gypsy Girl? That's not my name. I am Gypsy . . . just Gypsy. What I can do is go. I'll show young Knot Head what Gypsy can do.

The man started my engine—that blasted, useless engine—and backed me out of my slip. He forcefully turned my wheel hard over, blasted my rudder with a burst of water from the propeller, and I danced around sharply. Knot Head wasted no time and had my sails unfurled in seconds. The noisy engine fell silent before we'd left the marina, and we were *going.* I was beginning to like Knot Head.

He let me do things I didn't know I could do. We heeled twenty-five degrees, and I buried my starboard toe rail in the water. I'd never done that, but it felt good. I was *going.* I'd never gone that fast, and I wondered just how fast I could go.

We started a tack—

Equator! That's what the imaginary line around the middle of the Earth is called. The equator.

Anyway, we started a tack, turning my bow through the direction the wind was blowing, but Knot Head didn't release my headsail sheet. He had left my windward sheet cleated off and let my headsail backwind across my foredeck. We were heaving-to. I remembered that maneuver, but I hadn't done that since my sea trials the day I met my family.

Heaving-to is what a sailor does when he wants to stop me in the water without taking my sails down. My headsail tries to push me backward, and my mainsail tries to push me forward. The two forces cancel each other out, and I end up parked in the water, drifting very slowly downwind. That particular maneuver comes in handy in a storm, or if a sailor needs to go pee or make a sandwich.

Anyway, that's what we did. We *hove-to,* and I liked it. Knot Head knew how to sail.

He walked around on my deck, pulling and pushing on everything he could reach. He put his ear to my mast and listened. I have no idea what he was hoping to hear, but I loved that he was listening to me.

"You're a grand old girl. Aren't you, *Gypsy?*"

Hey! He got my name right. You bet I'm a grand old girl, Knot Head. What's going on with your hair, dude?

My new friend rolled me out of the heave-to and headed back toward the marina. I didn't want to go back. I wanted to *go*. I wanted to see what else Knot Head could have me do. I wanted to show off a little for him.

As we were sailing back, a boat that looked just like me sailed up beside us and slowly started passing us. I didn't like that at all. Anytime two sailboats are pointed in the same direction, that's a race.

Come on, Knot Head! You can't let them outrun us. You're better than that clown . . . even with your screwed-up hair.

I didn't know if he could hear me, or if we were just thinking the same thing, but he leapt to his feet and began trimming my sails. He'd stare upward into my rigging for a while and then at the other boat. Then he'd trim a little more. Then he'd stare and listen. Finally, he had my sails trimmed to perfection, and we sailed past that other boat that was trying to look so much like me, overtaking her by at least half a knot. She was cute enough, I suppose, but I was faster.

She chased us unsuccessfully all the way back to the marina, but Knot Head and I were victorious. To my surprise, her sailor looked a lot like mine. His hair was screwed-up, too. It must've been something in the water—wherever I was.

Knot Head quickly tied me back into the slip and leapt to the dock. The other sailor came running down the dock toward him. I hoped they weren't going to fight, but I was pretty sure Knot Head would win.

They didn't fight. Instead, they shook hands . . . or what could've been described as shaking hands, but it looked more like some sort of ridiculous hand dance. When it was over, both sailors looked me over with great interest.

"I love her already," said Knot Head.

"Yeah, man. I think she loves you, too. She's sure fast. Did you get a good deal on her?"

Deal? What's he talking about?

"Yeah, a great deal. A family up north had her since she was new, and I bought her for pennies on the dollar. They were giving up sailing. I got no idea why anybody would quit sailing, but I'm glad *Gypsy* fell in my lap."

"Congrats, man. I'm happy for you, but I'll beat you next time out."

Quit sailing? Bought her for pennies on the dollar? What is happening? What about my family?

Chapter 4
Friday

So much was going wrong, but I was curious about my new situation. Apparently, Knot Head was my new sailor, and I was his new boat. And wherever I was would apparently be my new home. Those two facts alone were enough to overwhelm me, but that's not what had my attention.

I'd seen other boats like me only once in my life. Sure, there were a lot of sailboats, and most of us looked similar, but to see one that looked so much like me was astonishing. My twin sister was tied up only a few hundred feet away, and I'd beaten her in a race. Well, I can't take all the credit. Knot Head and I had beaten her. I wanted to see her up close, and I wanted to race again.

My sailor came back, but he wasn't alone, and he wasn't empty-handed. He had a few friends and lots of stuff. He and his friends climbed aboard and set about cleaning and polishing every inch of me. It felt so good. I hadn't been thoroughly cleaned in so long, that I'd almost forgotten how it felt to sparkle. I felt brand-new again, but I still missed my family.

"What's her name, Trip?" someone on board asked.

Was *Trip* Knot Head's real name? That's a terrible name for a person. I couldn't call him Trip. I'd stick with Knot Head . . . KH for short.

"Her name's *Gypsy*, and I have no plans to change it." KH patted my wheel and stared up into my rigging.

"I think she's going to be happy here in Key West."

Key West? So that's where I am. All right, Key West. I can dig that. Now I want to go.

"Let's take her out, Trip."

I didn't know who had said that, but he must've read my mind.

"Done," said KH. "Cast off, and I'll fire up the engine."

Since KH apparently hated the diesel as much as I did, I knew it wouldn't be running for long. I was right. Just as before, KH backed me out of the slip and kicked my stern around with a quick propeller blast on the rudder, and up went my sails!

Oh, I love that feeling.

I heeled to starboard and gave KH all the speed I could muster. *Fast* is a relative term. Even though it may be painfully slow for a powerboat, seven knots is fast for a sailboat of my size. KH squeezed seven point three knots out of me, and I felt like a jet airplane. At least I assumed that's how a jet airplane must feel. It was great. My new sailor knew exactly how to get the most out of me, and best of all, he and his friends liked to clean me.

I felt a little guilty for being so happy. My family was sad and gone away, but I was having so much fun in the sun and warm water off Key West. Happiness should be celebrated, but mine was tempered with emptiness and loss. I think maybe it was okay for me to be happy, but I did miss my family, and selfishly, I hoped they missed me, too.

We sailed all afternoon, and even stopped at a place called Schooner Wharf Bar, where KH and all of his friends laughed, drank, ate, sang, and pointed their fingers at me while I was anchored in the warm water and sun. I think they were telling people about me and showing them which boat I was. There were so many boats of every shape and size. It was nice to have a sailor who liked talking about me and pointing me out to his new friends. Life in Key West was feeling good.

I was enjoying my afternoon swinging around on my anchor rode, a nautical term for the combination of chain and line that connects me to my anchor. *Line* is a silly little word for *rope*, but sailors hate the word *rope* for some reason. Hey, who was I to complain when a whole society of people called *mariners*—people of the sea—created a language just for me? I was flattered.

KH and his entourage came back, but this time they were in a beautiful little dinghy with a shiny, silver motor. The motor was much quieter than my diesel. I'll always hate my diesel. It was like a wart on my . . . well, I'll just stop there.

The dinghy was a Rigid Hulled Inflatable Boat, or RHIB for sort. She was beautiful and fast. I hoped we'd keep her. I'd always wanted one of my own.

KH helped his friends climb back aboard, and he tied the dinghy painter to my stern cleat. The painter is a small line to keep my dinghy from getting away. You know, kind of like a leash for a puppy. KH reached for the key to start my diesel, and I braced for the noise.

Someone said, "Hey, dude. I thought you were a sailor—not a powerboater. A real sailor wouldn't need the motor to get out of here."

Ah! A kindred spirit casting down a gauntlet.

I knew KH would rise to the challenge. He abandoned the key, looked up at the Windex, and smiled. I felt my headsail unfurl and my rudder come hard over. We were sailing off the mooring. KH was the best sailor in the world . . . but I was still worried about his hair.

We sailed out of the marina with the shiny RHIB trailing behind me. It was perfect. Everything was perfect.

It was a short sail back to the marina and my slip, but it was beautiful. The sunset was a collage of oranges and purples that danced across the Gulf of Mexico like ghostly spirits. The ocean reached up and embraced the sun, pulling it into its depths.

And that's when it happened.

I'd heard about it, but I'd thought it was just a legend. I'd had no idea it was real, but I saw it: an instantaneous flash of green just above the horizon as the sun disappeared. It was breathtaking.

"Did you see that, *Gypsy*? Did you see the green flash?"

KH was talking to me. He was actually talking to me.

Yeah, I saw it, Knot Head . . . I saw it.

"I've lived here for six years, and that's the first time I've ever seen it, *Gypsy*. Make a wish, old girl. Anything you wish for after seeing the green flash is going to come true."

Anything?

"I know what I wish. I wish Penelope were here."

Who's Penelope? Is she another boat? I'm your boat. I am Gypsy.

"Penelope is the most beautiful girl in the world, *Gypsy*. She's a lot like you. She's a classic beauty. She's fast when she wants to be, and she's soft and slow when she wants. Her eyes, *Gypsy* . . . my God, those eyes. They're like the ocean. You wouldn't believe those eyes . . . and that smile. Man, I miss her."

So, I can wish for anything—absolutely anything—and it'll come true?

KH pulled off his shirt and rolled it up to use as a pillow. He stretched out on my deck and stared into the darkening sky. The sounds from ashore were a cacophony of chaos. It was steel drums and guitars and people singing and talking. It was all happening, but it wasn't happening together. It was like every sound was battling against every other sound, but KH didn't seem to hear any of it.

How can he ignore all that noise?

I liked how he just lay there and stared up at the night sky. As the sun sank further and further beyond the darkened horizon, the sky overhead began to twinkle, first with a few faint stars, then finally, a canopy of brilliant, glimmering night-lights shone as if they were shining just for KH and me, and maybe for Penelope—whoever she was.

If I can really wish for anything and it'll come true, I think I wish for Penelope to come back to Trip. I think he loves her the way I love my family, and I'd sure love to have them come back. All of them . . . especially Tommy.

It felt funny thinking of my new sailor as Trip. Yeah, it was too weird. He'd always be Knot Head to me.

He slept on my deck, and I rocked in the gentle waves of the marina, enjoying my new home and sailor. He was comfortable with me, and I was happy to have him. I had no idea just how happy I could be until the same sun I'd watched disappear before the green flash, showed up again on the other side of the world the next morning.

Chapter 5

Saturday

"Hey, sailor! Permission to come aboard?"

A beautiful woman was standing on the dock beside me, tossing ice cubes at KH.

No . . . it couldn't be.

"Penelope? What are you doing here?" KH leapt to his feet and jumped to the dock as if he'd been shot from a cannon. He grabbed the woman, lifted her off her feet, and spun around like a crazy man. Her cup of ice flew from her hand, and a dozen seagulls dived on the pieces, hoping to find a morsel of something edible, but soon squawked away, disappointed.

I wasn't disappointed, though. It was Penelope. The wish after the green flash had worked. She'd come back from wherever she'd been. It was unbelievable, but it was happening, and it was real.

They kissed and held each other, giggling and laughing like children, until finally she said, "So, who's this new girl in your life?"

Oh no. It can't be true. Surely KH doesn't have someone new. Penelope is back, and she has to be the only one.

"This is *Gypsy*," he said, waving his hand across me and smiling like a proud new papa.

"She's breathtaking." Penelope pointed toward my deck. "May I?"

Yes, yes, yes, you absolutely may!

"Of course. Yes. You never need permission," he said.

He lifted her from her feet again and placed her gently on my deck.

She was barefoot and as graceful as a cat. She moved over my deck like her feet were made for me. I liked having her aboard.

"She's beautiful." Penelope said exactly what I was thinking. "Is she fun to sail?"

I held my breath, waiting for his answer.

"She's perfect. It's like she knows what I'm thinking, and she does it before I ask. I've never sailed any boat like her. You're gonna love her."

"I already do," she said, sliding her hand across my wheel.

He reached for her, and she sat on his lap, her arms draped across his tanned shoulders. She played with his knotted hair and laughed.

"Dreadlocks? Really?"

"Yeah, well, baby dreads for now. I had a lot to dread when you left."

"I'm back now."

"For good?"

"That's up to you." She traced the line of his jaw with her fingertips and pulled his face toward hers.

They kissed for a long time. I liked seeing people in love on my deck. It reminded me of how Thomas used to look at Terry so many years before. It was beautiful.

She shoved his face away from hers. "You really have to brush your teeth, sailor boy."

He covered his mouth and tried not to smile. "I'll be right back." He disappeared down my companionway and into the head to brush his teeth.

Oh, look, there's another nautical term. *Head* means bathroom on a boat. Believe it or not, sailors used to go to the very front of sailing ships and . . . well, you know . . . off the front of the ship, which they called the *head*. The name stuck for where people . . . well, you know . . . and to this day, the bathroom is the head.

Penelope rubbed her hands across my brightwork and winches, admiring me as much as I admired her. She was truly beautiful, and I understood why KH wanted her back.

I still couldn't believe that wishing thing after the green flash actually worked. I hoped I'd get to do that again someday.

"Feel like going for a sail?" KH poked his head, teeth glistening, through the companionway.

Penelope smiled. "Sure. Just let me get my things."

She leapt from my deck, onto the dock, and grabbed a big green duffle bag, a backpack, and a guitar case.

Oh, look. I think my theory about everyone having a guitar may be correct. I can't wait to hear her play . . . and maybe she'll sing for us.

KH helped her load her things aboard, and he cast off my lines. He went to work hoisting my mainsail right there in the slip. The wind was out of the east, so it was blowing right across my bow and down my deck.

He's going to sail me backward, right out of the slip. He's just showing off for Penelope, but I like it!

When my mainsail was fully aloft, he shoved the boom way out over my port rail, and the morning breeze started pushing us backward.

I'll tell you about boom and port rail in a minute.

I'd never been sailed backward before, and it felt weird, but just like everything else KH did, I wanted more of it. I wasn't built to sail backward, so nothing worked exactly right. But finally, he turned my wheel, and my rudder went to work bringing my stern around (remember, stern means my butt), and we sailed away from the marina without ever starting that nasty old diesel.

So, I promised to tell you about boom and port rail. My boom is a big metal bar that sticks out from the back of my mast, and it holds the foot of the mainsail. It's also what the mainsheet (the line used to trim my mainsail) is attached to, so it's pretty important. Port and starboard are left and right on a boat. I don't know if it's true, but I've heard that the terms originated hundreds of years before I was born, in sailing ships that carried cargo. The side of the ship that had a big hole in it to load cargo went toward the port, so it was called the port side. The other side had a big, long paddle called a steering board. I've heard that the steering board side was always opposite the port side and that somehow, through the years, even after some smart guy invented a rudder, sailors shortened steering board to starboard, and that became right, and port became left. I have no idea if any of that is true, but it's a good story, and who am I to let facts stand in the way of a good story?

The sun kept climbing into the sky, and the wind grew stronger. All of my sails were up and trimmed perfectly. It was a glorious day. Penelope held my wheel in her hand, but I didn't need much attention. The day was about KH and Penelope—not about me. I did my part to behave and let the two lovers reconnect.

"I can't believe you're back. So, what's up? Are you just taking a break from school, or what?"

She played with his baby dreads and tried to smile. "It just wasn't for me. I thought it was what I was supposed to do. You know, I'm just not cut out for college. I don't want to be an engineer or a lawyer. I just want to play and sing . . . and be with you."

She sings! I knew it. I can't wait to hear.

"What about your folks? They're going to be pissed."

"Yeah," she said, "they already are, but I can't live my life with them making decisions for me."

"I just can't believe you're back. It's too good to be true." Dread Head kissed her as if he never wanted to spend another second without her.

Nope, Dread Head doesn't work. I'm sticking with Knot Head.

"We really have to do something about your hair," said Penelope, pulling at the knots.

"Yeah, I know. It's terrible, isn't it?"

"It really is." She laughed and kissed him again.

Here come the dolphins. They always come at the best times.

"Look," Penelope whispered, pointing over my bow.

A pair of bottlenose dolphins leapt from the water in practiced, perfect unison, and pierced the surface without a hint of a splash.

They danced in my bow wave and kept leaping as if they were too excited to stay in the water. They were beautiful, just like Penelope and KH.

"Where do you want to go?" KH looked at her, his eyebrows raised.

She smiled at him. "Everywhere . . . with you!"

And that's exactly what we did. We went everywhere. It was the best year, ever.

They took such good care of me. They scrubbed my hull to keep me clean. It was amazing how quickly all sorts of stuff would grow on my hull in that hot tropical water. When the growth would build up, I'd get slow, and KH didn't like that, so he kept me as clean as a whistle. It made me laugh how the two of them would play a game to see who could hold their breath longer while cleaning my belly. Penelope always won. I think he let her win.

We went to The Bahamas. It was the most beautiful water—clear and blue. It tasted so clean, and there was so much to see. Sailing over the coral was like an ocean safari every day. There were billions of fish, and I saw my first octopus. She was amazing. She crawled up my rudder one night when we were anchored off Staniel Cay. I had no idea what she was, but she was quite the climber. She crawled right up over my stern and peered at Penelope.

"Well, hello there." She stood and stared, wide-eyed at the octopus resting on my stern. "Trip, check this out."

KH stuck his head out of my companionway and gasped. "Where did she come from?"

"The ocean would be my bet."

"See if she'll eat this, smart ass." He handed up a piece of lobster he'd been getting ready to grill.

She took it and carefully laid it on my coaming beside the unexpected guest. The octopus slowly and methodically curled one tentacle around the tasty morsel of lobster, then slid clumsily back into the sea. I'd never seen anything like it, and apparently, neither had Penelope or KH.

"What would make her come up here like that?"

"How should I know?" he said. "I had no idea they'd do that."

"You've got to admit, it was pretty cool."

"It was absolutely cool," he said.

And he was right. Cool it was, but it wasn't over. She was back, but this time, she wasn't empty-handed . . . or empty-tentacled. She delivered a piece of broken shell and carefully placed it where Penelope had placed the lobster bite. I assumed the octopus wanted to trade the shell for more lobster, but I was wrong. Only seconds after placing the shell on the deck, she slid over the rail and plopped back into the sea.

I was speechless . . . primarily because I'd never been able to speak, but even if I could have, I would've been speechless at that moment. I wasn't alone. KH and Penelope sat with their mouths agape, staring at the broken shell. Finally, they broke out in uproarious laughter, and KH grabbed the shell and headed down the companionway. A few minutes later, he came back with the shell laced on a thin leather string and tied it around Penelope's neck.

He knelt at her feet, took her hands in his, and said, "I don't have a ring to offer you. In fact, I don't have much of anything to offer you except my love and this beautiful broken shell from our friend, the octopus. But Penelope Ann Gibson, will you marry me?"

She cried, and I didn't understand. I'd seen people cry, but only when something terrible had happened. This wasn't terrible. This was good. This was fantastic, in fact.

I learned two things that evening anchored off Staniel Cay. I learned that an octopus is a very strange creature, and that there are two reasons people cry.

Penelope threw herself into KH's arms and told him she loved him a thousand times.

"Your love is all I want. As long as I have that, I'll have everything I need. Of course I'll marry you, but only if the octopus can come to the wedding."

I hoped it wasn't going to be my job to find the octopus and deliver the invitation. Not only was she strange, but she was a master of disguise. But once she hit the bottom, I never saw her again.

They were married on the beach a few days later. They were so much in love, and I got to see the whole thing.

It only got better from there. She played the guitar and sang more beautifully after that day. KH watched her swim in the ocean and admired everything about her. Sometimes they swam together, and I admired everything about them. They were so happy, and they would whisper *I love you* to each other. And just like Thomas and Terry, they made love in my forward cabin, and I didn't watch. I protected and embraced them, and I was their home, and they were my new family. And then the most wonderful thing happened —Penelope got fat.

KH talked to her belly, and then our family grew. A midwife came from St. Thomas, and Courtney Ellen Holiday was born in my main salon. It made a mess.

I didn't know that's how babies showed up, but it scared the crap out of me. Apparently, it was normal, because I was the only one freaked out. Baby Courtney was beautiful and the midwife cleaned up the mess . . . mostly.

So, Trip Holiday was my sailor's name . . . what an unfortunate name. Knot Head was so much better, even though Penelope had cut out the knots and left him with almost no hair. It eventually grew back, and it was normal hair, but he'd always be Knot Head to me. What a happy family we were: Penelope, Courtney, Knot Head, and Gypsy.

Chapter 6
Sunday

Everything always had to change just when it was getting great. I watched Courtney grow and learn to play and talk and eat without help. That was pretty amazing to see. In my last family, everyone could talk and eat when I met them. What an amazing life I was having.

I got to see my first family grow up, suffer unthinkable tragedy, and fall apart. Thinking back, it was sad to remember. I hoped they were safe and happy and healed someplace, but something made me doubt that would ever be possible for them.

I was watching my new family experience everything wonderful. We were traveling and seeing amazing things, and Courtney was perfect. And then it happened again. Penelope got fat.

KH talked to her tummy again, but this time, no midwife came. Instead, everyone left, and I was all alone in an anchorage in San Juan, Puerto Rico. I could smell the rum distillery, and I liked that, but I missed my family. The sun went up and down four times while they were gone, and I was afraid it was happening again. I was afraid they were getting tired of me and would only come back now and then—just like my first family—and that I would get dirty and broken again. I was afraid and lonely.

They came back, all four of them, but what happened next terrified me.

"It breaks my heart to even consider being without Gypsy, but I think you're probably right. She's just not big enough for all four of us."

What? Yes, I am! I'm big enough. I am! Take out that diesel. We don't need that thing. That'll make plenty of room.

"We don't have to make any decisions today. It's just something we have to think about."

Penelope stepped aboard with the new baby in her arms. "Look, Ocean, this is Gypsy. She's our home."

Oh, they named the baby Ocean. That's perfect. And she called me their home. That's the best thing I've ever been called.

I was busy watching Ocean and didn't notice KH untying my lines. Before I knew it, we were out of the slip and sailing out of Bahìa de San Juan. The wind blew perfectly for Ocean's first sail, and dolphins came to see her.

She giggled and cooed, and blinked her eyes when the sun shone on her. She was so beautiful. She looked just like Courtney when she was a baby, but without the mess in my main salon.

We sailed for hours, but not like we used to sail. KH was careful and gentle. He didn't let me *go* like he used to, and I didn't want to run. I wanted Ocean's first time on the water to be perfect. We could *go* fast some other time . . . if there would be some other time.

A few nights later, it happened. I'd been dreading the talk, but I knew it was coming. KH sat on my deck and leaned back against my mast, rubbing his hand across me.

"*Gypsy*, old girl, we've had quite a time together. We saw the green flash together. Remember that?"

Yeah, I remember. How could I forget? We both wished for Penelope, and she came back. I need to see another green flash so I can wish for us to stay together.

"You're the best old boat there is, *Gypsy*, and I love you."

If I were capable of tears, they would've been coming. It was hard to hear KH tell me goodbye. I wondered where I'd go. What would become of me? Would I get a new family? Would I ever see Ocean and Courtney again?

"I've found you a great new home. My granddad is coming to get you. You'll love him. He's just like you, *Gypsy*. He's spent his whole life on the water. It's all he knows. He's grouchy sometimes, but he's going to love you, and he'll take really great care of you. Me and Penelope are taking a job at a resort here in San Juan, and we're getting a real house. It'll never be a home like you are, but it'll be good for the girls. And it wouldn't be fair for you to have to sit in the marina all the time. You're a sailboat, *Gypsy*. You need to be out there sailing, and granddad will take you sailing every day."

I was sad and happy at the same time, and that didn't make any sense to me. I was happy that my family was getting a real house and a job. San Juan seemed like a nice place for a family. They had a rum distillery and a castle. That was a good start.

KH sat there for a long time. I don't know what he was thinking, or if he was thinking anything at all, but I liked just spending those last few minutes with him. He'd been a great part of my life. He'd taught me how much fun it was to live life on the edge, to push myself to *go* faster, and to not be afraid to sail across the horizon to places I'd never been. I learned that life is about more than comfort and safety; sometimes it's about feeling alive and throwing caution to the wind. But I also learned that it's about loving someone else and creating new life with that person, then falling in love over and over again with your family, and building something bigger and stronger than that free-spirited existence. It's about discovering what's important at every stage of life. That's what I learned from Knot Head.

When the sun came up the next morning, Penelope sat on my deck with her bare feet hanging over the starboard toe rail.

"I love you, *Gypsy*. I'm really going to miss you. You welcomed me, you shared Trip with me, and you did it with such grace and style. You're a real treasure, *Gypsy*. Thank you for being my home, and a home for my children. I'll see you again. It won't be long." And she cried. I wanted to cry, too.

Penelope proved that real life isn't about doing what others expect or think you should do. Real life is about being true to the part of you that makes you happy. I think that part is your heart. Penelope proved that college isn't for everyone, and that some people are happiest when they find their way back to whom and what they truly love, and then they build something perfect and wonderful—like a family. That's what I learned from Penelope.

Courtney sat in my cockpit with Ocean squirming and cooing. A dragonfly landed on Ocean's toe, and Courtney giggled.

"Look, Ocean. You've got a new friend."

The whole world was an adventure for Courtney. Everything was exciting, and having a new baby sister to share that excitement with was the best thing she'd ever known. People need innocence and fascination, and they need someone to share that with. The world is full of dragons and flies, but dragonflies are rare and make really great new friends. That's what I learned from Courtney and Ocean.

Nothing could've prepared me for what I would learn next, or for the person I'd learn it from. KH's granddad showed up. It's going to take a while to describe him.

Describing how he looked is far less important than describing how he was. He held Ocean in his enormous, weathered, crooked hands, and tears rolled down his aged cheeks. Ocean reached for his white beard and giggled. They were seventy-five years apart but connected by something beautiful and timeless. They instinctually loved each other without choice or decision.

Courtney climbed on the old man's lap and told him everything she knew about everything, and he listened as if she were the only voice in the universe. They played and laughed and talked, and I'd never seen anything like it.

Penelope played her guitar and sang for Granddad, and he danced with Courtney on my deck while she stood on his feet. They cooked and ate on my deck, and it reminded me of the times with my first family when we'd anchor out and do the same thing. Perhaps cooking and eating and just being together has some value that can't be rightfully defined . . . perhaps.

Penelope and the girls went to sleep, and KH and Granddad sat on my deck sipping a cocktail. Granddad pulled out a cigar and stuck it in his mouth. It smelled magnificent. I'd seen cigars before, but never up close, and I'd never smelled one that smelled so good.

"She's a beautiful boat, son. You don't know how much it means to me that you want me to have her."

"Yeah, she's a great boat. I can't think of anyone who'd take better care of her than you. She's been my home and my family's home for a long time. I just couldn't swallow the thought of her going to somebody who'd mistreat her."

KH loved me and he wanted me to be happy and safe and well cared for. I loved him, too. And I wanted exactly the same for him.

Granddad pointed his cigar at KH. "I'll take care of her, but you've got to let me pay you for her. I can't just take your boat."

"You're not paying me for her, and that's all we're going to say about that. I want you to have her, and she needs someone like you to look after her."

"You're a stubborn kid . . . just like your grandmother was."

I watched KH swallow a lump in his throat. "I miss her, Granddad."

"Yeah, son, me too. She was the best of 'em. She always kept that home fire burning while I was gone for all those years. I should've been home more, but my life was out here on the water. It was where I belonged. It's all I've ever known. Your grandmother deserved better than an old salt like me."

They sat in silence for a long time until the old man finally said, "Well, let's get some sleep, and I'll play with those grandbabies of mine in the morning before me and old *Gypsy* here head north."

"Good night, Granddad."

The sun came up just like it always does, and Granddad was sitting on the dock with a white fluffy puppy in his hands when Courtney came up on deck.

"Ooh! A puppy!"

"He's for you," said the old man, "but there's one condition."

"What's a condition?" She took the puppy in her arms. He licked her face, and she laughed and danced like a little princess.

I remembered thinking that Tina was a princess, but she'd grown up to be so sad and empty. I hoped Courtney and her new puppy would never grow up.

"A condition is something that you have to do for me."

"Okay, Granddad. I'll do anything for you," she said, still dancing with the puppy.

He handed Courtney a small brown bag. "Wait until I'm gone, and then give this to your daddy. Can you do that that?"

"Sure I can. No problem." She peeled open the top of the bag and peered inside. "It's money. Lots of money."

"Yes, it's money that I want your daddy and mommy to have, but they won't take it from me. So, I want you to give it to them when I'm gone, and in return, you can keep the puppy. Do we have a deal?"

"You betcha!"

Chapter 7
Monday

"You know, my name's not really Granddad. You can call me Cappy. I started out as a deckhand on a tugboat sixty years ago, and I ain't never done nothing else."

Was he talking to me?

We were sailing north from San Juan, but I didn't know where we were going. It was just him and me, so I guess he must have been talking to me.

"I worked my way up to deck boss and then to engineer. Man oh man, did I think I'd made the big time when they made me engineer."

He didn't sail me like KH. He was careful and didn't push me too hard. I was getting old, but I still liked to *go* sometimes. Although, I liked the way he babied me . . . and how he talked to me.

"Didn't take long for me to hate them old diesels, though. They're noisy and greasy, and damn it's hot down in them engine rooms."

I know exactly how you feel!

"So, I found a sack of books about how to navigate and steer and figure out weather. I read them books about a hundred times, and I figured I'd go on up to the pilothouse and see if the old man would let me drive a little. They made me an apprentice mate, and he let me steer."

He pulled another cigar from his pocket and lit it. I liked the smell even more out on the open ocean.

So, what happened next?

"Oh, yeah. I was telling you about learning to steer."

Holy crap! I think he can hear me.

"It turned out I's pretty good at runnin' the old boat. I knew all about the deck work and the engines, so it made pretty good sense to me."

I still don't understand why I'm supposed to call you Cappy.

"It wasn't long after that, the company made me captain of an old tug, and I had my own crew. They were a good crew, but they were young and green. We kinda learned the ropes together. I'd teach 'em what I knew, and they caught on pretty quick. I reckon we surprised a lot of folks. We had the sorriest old tug in the yard and the greenest crew and the newest captain, but we sure got a lot of work done. The crew took to callin' me Cappy, and it just stuck."

He stood and stretched, making sounds like he was falling apart. I liked his stories, and I liked Cappy. He left me to my own devices and went below. When he came back on deck, he had a sandwich and big bottle of beer.

"This ain't really a beer. It's just a beer bottle. I won't be drinking when we're out here like this. It's just water in a beer bottle. I promise. Here, see for yourself."

He poured out a little from the bottle and let it run across my deck and into my scuppers. Sure enough, it was just water.

Oh, I guess you probably don't know what scuppers are. They're little slits that let water run off a boat so the decks and cockpit won't hold water. We boats are pretty amazing things.

"I had a pretty good run of it for sixty years or so. I pushed barges and dragged big ships all over the world. I guess you and me have got a lot in common. I ain't never seen any place that wasn't touching the water. Have you?"

No, I didn't know there are places that don't touch the water. That just seems weird.

"You know, *Gypsy*, maybe the parts of the world that don't touch the water are better. But I guess we'll never know, will we?"

No, Cappy. We probably won't, and that's okay with me.

"Yeah, that's just fine with me. If it ain't salty, I ain't interested."

We sailed on and on, stopping most nights so Cappy could sleep. He was a good sailor, and he took good care of me. We finally made it all the way to Panama City, Florida, not too far from where I was born. It was a lot different than the Caribbean, but I liked life there with Cappy.

I got to meet a lot of his old crew. Blister Foot was my favorite. He didn't wear shoes, and I like people who don't wear shoes. Believe it or not, he had a guitar.

"You old barefooted fool. What are you doing here?"

"Hey, Cappy. It's good to see you, too. Can I come aboard?"

"If you brought rum you can."

Blister Foot held up a bottle of Captain Morgan and climbed over my starboard lifeline.

They talked and drank and laughed about how things used to be. "How long's it been, Cappy?"

"Oh, I don't know. Fifteen minutes or fifteen years . . . it's all the same to me anymore."

Blister Foot said, "Yeah, I know exactly what you mean." He picked up his guitar, strummed a few chords, and started to sing.

"Fifteen minutes or fifteen years. It's hard to tell the difference, and nobody cares anymore."

That's when another guy showed up with an old beat-up guitar with only five strings. "Hey, you mind if I sit in and pick a little?"

"Sure, come on up. I'm Blister Foot and this is Cappy."

"Nice to meet you both. I'm Charlie. I used to write a little music back in the day."

Charlie came up, and he made that poor old five-stringed guitar sing. He told stories about writing songs with Elvis and how his brother was a big country music star.

People came strolling by on the dock, and some of them waved and spoke, but some of them stopped and sang along when they knew the words.

It was marina life, and it was a good life—a good life for Cappy and me. I spent a lot of time thinking about what I'd seen and heard in my life. I often wondered where my first family—Thomas, Terry, and Tina—was, and if I'd ever see them again. I thought about Knot Head and Penelope and their two beautiful daughters, Courtney and Ocean. I hoped they liked living in their house and having their job at the resort. Something made me think they probably wished they were still living on a boat and making deals with an octopus who trades lobster for broken shells. What a time we had.

That's when I saw Papa, and I knew something was wrong. His name wasn't really Papa, but he looked like the pictures of Ernest Hemingway I'd seen, so I thought of him as Papa. He had a big white beard, and he always seemed to be in charge. That sounds a lot like Hemingway, don't you think?

Anyway, he was the harbormaster, and he was walking the docks wearing a look I didn't like. He was frowning, and his brow was wrinkled as if he just couldn't find anything to be happy about.

"Hey, Cappy," he yelled as he approached.

Cappy stuck his head out of my companionway. "Oh, hey, Greg. How's it going this morning?"

"Not so good, Cappy. Have you been listening to the weather?"

"Yeah, I listened yesterday, but I've slept since then. There was a little tropical storm twisting up down south of Cuba. That's the only thing I heard."

"Yeah, well, it's turning into a hurricane, and it's headed this way. Have you got a plan?"

Cappy turned and eyed the sky to the south. If the storm was still south of Cuba, it had a long way to come to get to Panama City, but that didn't stop Cappy from trying to see some sign of it in the sky.

"Hmm, a hurricane you say? I don't like the sound of that."

"Yeah, you probably ought to come up with a plan," said Papa. "Let me know if you need anything. I'm going to wake up the rest of the old guys."

"Good luck to you," said Cappy.

"Yeah, you too."

Cappy turned and looked back toward the south and chewed on the corner of his bottom lip. "Hmm, a hurricane," I heard him whisper with a raspy hint of concern.

I'd heard about hurricanes, and I knew they were bad, but I'd never actually seen one. I knew Cappy would know what to do. We'd be safe.

He flipped on the VHF radio and tuned into the NOAA weather station. Papa had been right. It was a category one hurricane, and it was moving north at fourteen knots. It was expected to become a category three by the time it made landfall. I didn't know exactly what that meant, but I knew that one hundred thirty mile per hour wind was going to suck.

I heard Cappy on the phone trying to find a boatyard who had room to haul me out and put me up on blocks where I'd be safe. I didn't like the sound of that. It sounded painful to me, but I trusted Cappy.

It turned out not to matter since all the boatyards were either full or had run out of stands. Boats started leaving the marina, and everybody looked scared. People were boarding up windows and taking everything that wasn't tied down off the docks.

"I'll be back, *Gypsy*. Don't you worry. I'm not going to let anything happen to you." Cappy hopped onto the dock as if he were twenty-five years old again and headed up the ramp. I didn't know where he was going, but he wasn't abandoning me. He wouldn't do that.

When he came back, he had two buckets of chain, a huge anchor, and a bunch of bottled water. He lugged everything aboard and went to work. He worked all day, rigging my new anchor and chain, and taking down my canvas and sails. Apparently, he didn't want anything to get blown off when the hurricane came.

He never turned the radio off. It just kept repeating the same ominous forecast over and over until the monotonous recording changed. Everyone on the dock and on nearby boats froze.

". . . Hurricane Michael, now a category two, is expected to make landfall between Destin and Apalachicola as a category three hurricane with winds in excess of one hundred twenty miles per hour. Storm surge of eight to ten feet possible with damaging flooding likely. Residents are encouraged to evacuate or seek shelter . . ."

Cappy patted my mast with his calloused hand. "Don't worry, old girl, I'll be right here with you."

He went back to work, making sure there was nothing loose in my rigging that could give way during the storm. He provisioned the lockers with enough water and food to last for weeks. I was starting to get scared. I had faith that Cappy would protect me, but he even looked concerned.

By the time Cappy had done everything he could to get me ready to move out of the marina, my barometer had started acting strange. The barometric pressure was dropping like a rock. Something nasty was on its way. It was eerie to see all the other boats leaving the marina. I wondered where they were going, and I wondered if they were scared, too.

"We've got quite an adventure ahead of us, Gypsy. Let's get some sleep while we can, old girl."

Cappy crawled into my forward cabin that night, but I don't think he got much sleep.

Chapter 8
Tuesday

The sun came up just as it always did, and the sky looked like any normal day, but nothing normal was going on around me.

Papa was back. "Cappy, you can leave the boat here in the marina, but I can't let you stay onboard. You have to find someplace to go."

Cappy looked at the sky. "No, I won't be leaving her here. I'll find a nice hurricane hole for her somewhere, and we'll ride it out together."

"That's up to you, Cappy, but they're saying it might be a category four by the time it gets here tomorrow."

"Is that right? A category four, huh?"

"That's what they're saying," mumbled Papa.

"That's one-thirty-one to one-fifty-five, ain't it?"

"Yeah, Cappy, it is. That's a real storm."

Cappy grabbed my winch as if he were holding on for his life. "It's gonna be one for the history books, I reckon."

"Yeah, it is. Do you need anything, Cappy? I'm going to be heading home soon to see what I can do to get the house ready."

"No. I've got everything I need. Good luck to you, Greg."

"You too, Cappy."

Papa walked away, but he looked back twice. I don't know what he was thinking, but I suspect he was wondering if he'd ever see me and Cappy again.

"I'll be back, *Gypsy*. Don't you leave without me."

Cappy climbed up on the dock, looking every day of his age. He disappeared, and I secretly hoped he wouldn't come back. I didn't know what was coming, but everybody was scared. I wanted Cappy to be safe. He didn't need to be out in that storm. He needed to be someplace that didn't touch the water . . . someplace that wasn't salty. But I knew he'd be back.

Just like I knew he would, he came back with biscuit crumbs in his beard and a big to-go cup of black coffee. He also had two big diesel cans with him, and he poured the fuel into my tank, even though I didn't want it. Maybe diesel was like coffee.

My sails were gone. Cappy had taken them down and stowed them away in a locker below my deck. Anywhere we went was going to be because of that nasty, noisy, stinky diesel. I guessed maybe I needed that engine, after all.

We motored out of the marina and things just kept getting more and more eerie. There were no birds. The big pelicans who usually dived on bait just outside the marina were nowhere in sight. The seagulls who squawked and begged for every morsel they could find were missing.

The wind had picked up enough to produce ominous whitecaps on the bay. A few dolphins scurried about, but even they seemed to know something was wrong.

One of the huge navy ships was anchored out in the middle of the bay. Behind that ship, a line of big sailboats also at anchor tugged at their moorings in the twenty-knot precursor to the worst storm any of us had ever seen. Anchoring in the open was the only possibility of survival. Remaining in the marina meant certain destruction against the rigid docks and unforgiving rocks of the shore. For the big boats, that was an option, but not for me.

Those boats weighed fifty thousand pounds or more. That's more than twice what I weighed. Their rigging was heavier and their hulls were thicker. The safety they expected from the open bay would be almost as bad for me as the rocks on the shore. Cappy was taking me someplace safe, I hoped.

"I think we'll go to Pearl Bayou. What do you think, *Gypsy*?"

He was asking me where I thought we should anchor to survive the storm together. I didn't know what was best, so I silently trusted him.

We watched other boats motor into other bayous and sloughs, and Cappy looked longingly into those coves, obviously wondering if those were better, safer options. Ultimately, we motored on.

Pearl Bayou was almost full of boats of every description. There were bizarre sailboats with three hulls, and even double-enders whose sterns looked like bows. There were powerboats, and even a big ketch.

A ketch is a gorgeous boat that can do a lot of things I couldn't do. It has two masts—a main mast and a mizzen mast— and can carry three sails and be trimmed in a thousand different ways to make its family comfortable onboard.

I'd never be a ketch, but I was tall and proud, even though I only had one mast and two sails. But ultimately, none of that mattered when a category four hurricane was less than twenty-four hours away.

We motored through the maze of boats, and Cappy finally picked a spot in the back of the bayou. It was just deep enough so my keel wouldn't get stuck in the mud, and just wide enough to put out plenty of anchor rode so I could swing around when the wind changed directions. I wondered why no one else had chosen that spot. It was like they'd been saving it just for me.

Cappy put out the big, heavy anchor and let the chain follow it to the bottom. He tied it off and let me drift back a dozen feet before letting more chain slide into the water. Over and over, he repeated the process until he'd let out two hundred feet of chain. Next came a bridle, a pair of heavy nylon straps that held the anchor chain to my bow.

The diesel came back to life, and I braced myself for the strain that was coming. Cappy pulled my transmission into reverse and began to back down on the anchor. He pulled hard against the anchor chain so the anchor would bury itself deeply in the muddy bottom of the bayou, and hopefully stay there through the storm. With my diesel pulling as hard as it could, we stopped moving, and

I felt myself shudder as my propeller tried to keep pulling us backward but couldn't overcome the anchor. I felt securely anchored and my diesel fell silent.

Then something strange happened. Cappy started talking to someone else. He wasn't talking to me, and he wasn't using the radio or telephone. There was no one else aboard, yet he was still talking.

"You know I ain't never asked you for much," I heard him say, "but there ain't nothing normal about any of this. I'd really appreciate it if you'd see fit to keep me and *Gypsy* safe through this thing. I'd like to see them grandbabies again, and me and *Gypsy's* got a lot left to talk about. So, look after us if you would. Amen."

Who's he talking to? Whoever it is, I hope he was listening.

There was no green flash that night, but the sunset was astonishing and wholly unforgettable. The purples consumed the sky while dancing and rolling with reds and oranges that longed to embrace the ever-darkening heavens. The sun seemed to fear the coming storm would devour even her, so she poured herself across the canvas of sky, painting, perhaps, the final sunset there would ever be.

Chapter 9
Wednesday

The wind blew all night and was steadily getting stronger, but it wasn't bad when the sun finally came up the next morning. It was blowing around forty knots, but I'd seen that much wind in the Caribbean. I still didn't know what to expect, and Cappy was unusually quiet.

He checked and rechecked every inch of me, making sure I was as ready as I could be. He assembled what he'd called a ditch bag. He put in water, food, a telephone, a radio, money, a change of clothes, and bug spray, even though there were no bugs. Even the bugs knew the storm was coming.

Cappy tied his ditch bag to a big white fender, and then tied the whole thing off to a cleat at my stern. He tied a little slip knot that he could quickly pull loose if he needed.

I was in good hands, but that hurricane was getting closer every minute.

The sky turned ugly, and I could hear sounds that I'd never heard. Pine trees were swaying and rubbing together, making eerie sounds. The wind howled and the rain began. Alarms and sirens wailed in the distance. The weather radio announced that Hurricane Michael would make landfall near Tyndall Air Force Base as a category four hurricane, with sustained winds of one hundred fifty-five miles per hour.

The entrance to Pearl Bayou lies on the edge of Tyndall Air Force Base . . . exactly where we were anchored.

Cappy pulled on his foul weather gear and the biggest life jacket I'd ever seen. I didn't even know I had a life jacket like that onboard. He wedged himself into a corner of my cockpit and pressed his feet against the gunwale.

The sky burst open, and all the wind in the world descended upon us. Walls of water poured from the boiling sky. The air filled trees and water and wind, and it was impossible to see. Cappy was wearing goggles to protect his eyes, but they were useless. The relentless walls of water and wind crushing against us, wave after wave, was unbearable.

My anchor chain strained and begged to break, but it would not. The heavy anchor drove itself deeper into the mud and held on with mighty strength. We rolled violently until my mast slapped the water so hard I felt my keel shudder from the force.

Cappy was thrown about like a rag doll, his body arching and bending and twisting every time he struck my deck. I could barely hear his agonizing cries over the roaring, rushing wind and relentless water.

There was no sky, and there was no sea. It was all the same. Everything I'd known vanished into a howling, liquid chaos.

I felt parts of myself fail and fly away, riven by the unimaginable force of the storm. One moment, my mast would be underwater to port, or what I believed to be port, and the next second, I'd be on my side to starboard. I bucked and lunged against my mooring, but I couldn't break free. If only I could break free and ease the agony of the relentless pull of the chain and anchor. If only. . . .

And then I heard it. It was the chain surrendering under the immeasurable force. I should've been free, and the agony should've soon ended, but it didn't end—and I wasn't free. I was still shackled to the bottom of the bayou that was to have been my refuge, but had become my hell.

What snapped? What did I hear?

My question was silenced by a horrible answer. The ketch I had so admired had snapped her mooring and was now crushing herself against my bow. Splinters of every imaginable substance—fiberglass, wood, iron, steel—exploded into the liquid air above my deck. The enormous main mast of the ketch came collapsing like a mighty oak, ripping at my rigging and tearing away at what was left of me.

The force of the collision with the ketch mercifully ripped me from my mooring and sent me tumbling, keel over mast, mast over keel, until neither remained.

As we collided, the body of a man who could've been KH or Thomas or a thousand others, came melting across my deck and pouring into my cockpit with Cappy. The man wore no life jacket and showed no signs of life. Cappy, broken and crawling through death's gaping door, twisted free of his life jacket, and in a desperate, final selfless act, he tied the jacket to the man's body. Seconds later, they were both swept overboard from what was left of my crumbling, failing deck. The two bodies vanished in the blackened void that had been sky and air, but was now a lifeless chasm of turmoil and chaos.

For hours upon hours, the storm raged and howled and annihilated all that had been before it. I succumbed to the force and rage, as did every other thing, alive or not, within what I had known to be the world around me. Nothing remained as it had been. Everything was slaughtered and trodden and emptied of wholeness, and left broken, bent, and defeated.

What remained of me was but splinters and tangled, indistinguishable bits of rubbish and destruction. Cappy was no more, but the man who now wore Cappy's life jacket, sat whimpering and gasping against the broken, shattered hull of a boat I'd never seen, resting a hundred feet away in a cluster of decimated trees. The man was alive because Cappy had chosen to give his life to save another. That is what humanity should be. That is what I learned from Cappy.

As I succumb to the forces of the storm that I lacked the strength to overcome, I remember the love I have for my families. I remember how I grew in spirit as I watched them grow, and how I experienced the heartbreaks they endured. I remember the adventures we had and the trials we faced together. I remember how they looked at me the first time they saw me, and how much I treasured their touch and affection. They trusted and love me, and I adored every one of them. I hope they all know that had it been required of me, I would have lovingly and willingly given my life for any of them. I would have, without hesitation, allowed myself to be torn plank from plank, and stem from stern, so they could have one last bit of me to cling to—so that some small piece of me might hold them afloat as the world dissolved around them. No greater honor could I have been given than to be what they needed so desperately when fear overwhelmed them. I would have done so because I love them . . . each of them. And as I surrender now to my wounds, my dying desire is for my family to know that I loved them completely.

I was Gypsy.

About the Author

Cap Daniels

Cap Daniels is a sailing charter captain, scuba and sailing instructor, pilot, Air Force veteran, and civil servant of the U.S. Department of Defense. Raised far from the ocean in rural East Tennessee, his early infatuation with salt water was sparked by the fascinating, and sometimes true, sea stories told by his father, a retired Navy Chief Petty Officer. Those stories of adventure on the high seas sent Cap in search of adventure of his own which eventually landed him on Florida's Gulf Coast where he owns and operates a sailing charter service and spends as much time as possible on, in, and under the waters of the Emerald Coast.

Visit *www.CapDaniels.com* to sign up for the mailing list to receive updates on coming novels, future release dates, and my newsletter.

Connect on Facebook @WriterCapDaniels

Other Works by Cap Daniels

Chase Fulton Novels:
Book One: The Opening Chase
Book Two: The Broken Chase
Book Three: The Stronger Chase
Book Four: The Unending Chase – Winter 2018/19

www.ingramcontent.com/pod-product-compliance
Lightning Source LLC
Chambersburg PA
CBHW020320150626
46552CB00022B/3021